![Daniel Tiger's Neighborhood]

Daniel Meets the New Neighbors

Adapted by Becky Friedman
Based on the screenplay "Won't You Be Our Neighbor?"
written by Jill Cozza-Turner & Becky Friedman
Poses and layouts by Jason Fruchter

Simon Spotlight
New York   London   Toronto   Sydney   New Delhi

SIMON SPOTLIGHT
An imprint of Simon & Schuster Children's Publishing Division
1230 Avenue of the Americas, New York, New York 10020
This Simon Spotlight paperback edition August 2018
© 2018 The Fred Rogers Company
All rights reserved, including the right of reproduction in whole or in part in any form.
SIMON SPOTLIGHT and colophon are registered trademarks of Simon & Schuster, Inc.
For information about special discounts for bulk purchases, please contact
Simon & Schuster Special Sales at 1-866-506-1949 or business@simonandschuster.com.
Manufactured in the United States of America 0819 LAK
10 9 8 7 6 5 4 3
ISBN 978-1-5344-2962-8
ISBN 978-1-5344-2963-5 (eBook)

It was a beautiful day in the Neighborhood of Make-Believe when Daniel noticed something different! It was a truck . . . and not just any truck. It was a *big* truck with *big* boxes inside.

"Why is that truck there?" Daniel asked Dad Tiger.

"That's a moving truck," said Dad Tiger. "New neighbors must be moving in to the house next door."

"New neighbors?" said Daniel. "I wonder if there will be a new friend for me!"

"What's inside all those boxes?" Daniel asked.

"You have to pack up all your clothes and toys and furniture when you move," Mom Tiger explained.

"I wonder what it would be like to move to a different house," Daniel said. Daniel imagined that he was moving!

Just then Daniel noticed that one of the boxes was shaking!

"Look! Someone is carrying that box!" said Daniel. "Who is it?"

Daniel couldn't see who was carrying the box. All he could see were two little feet.

"Come on, Daniel," said Mom Tiger. "Let's go over and meet the new neighbors!"

"Okay!" said Daniel. "Maybe I'll meet a new friend!"

Daniel rang the doorbell. *Ding-dong!*

"Hello!" said Mom Tiger when the door opened. "We're your neighbors, the Tiger family. Welcome to the neighborhood!"

"Thank you!" said the neighbor. "I'm Dr. Platypus, but you can call me Dr. Plat!"

Daniel introduced himself. "I'm Daniel, and this is my sister, Margaret. I've never met a platypus before."

"You haven't?" said Dr. Plat. "That's very exciting then, isn't it? Please, come inside!"

Daniel, Mom Tiger, and Margaret followed her inside the house.

The Platypus house looked different from Daniel's house. There was no furniture—just boxes everywhere! As Daniel looked around, he heard a rustle from a nearby box! Could that be a new friend for him? Daniel looked around the room until . . .

"Peekaboo!" said a little boy.
And then another little boy appeared!
"Peekaboo!" said the second boy.
Daniel couldn't believe his eyes. They looked the same!

"Meet Teddy and Leo! They're twins!" said Dr. Plat. "That means they are two kids from the same family who were born on the same day." Margaret toddled over to Teddy and Leo, and they started to play. "Margaret has two new friends, but what about me?" said Daniel.

Then Daniel heard a giggle! *Is there someone else here?* he wondered.

Daniel looked around until he found another platypus! But this time it was a girl.

"I'm Jodi," she said shyly before quickly running out of the room.

Maybe Jodi will be my friend, Daniel thought.

Daniel and Jodi went to her room.
"This is my room," said Jodi, "but there are so many boxes."
"I can help you unpack!" said Daniel.
Jodi smiled. "Okay."

Daniel helped Jodi unpack her toys and stuffed animals.
"This is Benji the hedgehog!" said Jodi. "He likes to sing!"
"*Mi, mi, mi!*" sang Daniel.

Daniel and Jodi put her special pillow called a cozi-cozi on her bed.
"I've never seen a cozi-cozi before," said Daniel, "but it is comfy!"

Dr. Plat brought in two cribs.

"Why do you have cribs in your room?" asked Daniel.

"Because Teddy and Leo sleep in here, too!" explained Jodi.

"That sounds like fun!" said Daniel.

When Daniel and Jodi were done unpacking, they decided to draw some pictures together.

"I always carry crayons," said Jodi.

Daniel was learning a lot about Jodi.

The doorbell rang. It was Mr. McFeely!

"Speedy delivery for our new neighbors!" he said, handing Dr. Plat an envelope. "Everyone is invited to a welcome party at the Enchanted Garden today!"

Daniel was very excited. "Did you hear that, Jodi? You're going to love the Enchanted Garden!"

"Wait!" said Jodi. "We can't go!" She looked very upset.

"What's wrong, Jodi?" asked Daniel.

"We can't go to the party because I can't find my special book!" said Jodi. "Mama reads it to me every night. I can't go to bed without it, and if I can't find it, then I don't want to go to the party."

Daniel was worried. He didn't want Jodi to be upset!

"I'll help you find your book," Daniel offered.

Daniel helped Jodi look . . .

and look . . .

and look for her book everywhere.

But they still couldn't find it!
"Maybe we should look outside," suggested Daniel.
Jodi agreed.
So Daniel, Jodi, and Dr. Plat all went outside to look for Jodi's special book.

Daniel looked around outside until he noticed a book peeking out from under a bush! It was a Tigey the Adventure Tiger Book.

"Is this your book, Jodi?" he asked.

"Yes!" said Jodi happily. "Thank you, Daniel Tiger!"

"You're welcome," said Daniel. "I love Tigey the Adventure Tiger, too!"

"I'm so glad to have a neighbor just like you," said Daniel. "I'm so glad to have a *friend* just like you," said Jodi. "Let's go to the party!" Daniel said.

When Jodi and her family got to the party, the whole neighborhood was there.

"Welcome to the neighborhood!" they said.

"Thank you!" said Jodi.

Daniel smiled. "I think you're going to like it here."

And Jodi and her family had the best time getting to know their new neighbors . . . and friends.

"We have a new neighbor in the neighborhood. Her name is Jodi! I think she's going to like it here, don't you? I like that you're my neighbor, too. Ugga Mugga."

Do you want to learn more about
being a good neighbor?
Read on for some helpful advice
from Daniel Tiger and his friends.

You can welcome new neighbors in your own special way!

Everyone in the Neighborhood of Make-Believe was so excited when the Platypus family arrived! Each neighbor wanted to welcome the new family in their own special way.

- Daniel and his family wanted to give sunflowers to the Platypus family.

- Baker Aker wanted to give banana bread.

- King Friday and Queen Sara wanted to say a royal hello.

- Mr. McFeely wanted to deliver the Platypus family's very first letter.

- O the Owl wanted to read with the Platypus family.

- Miss Elaina wanted to play ball with them.

- Katerina wanted to dance with them.

- Prince Wednesday wanted to show them his rock collection.

If new neighbors moved into your neighborhood, how would you want to welcome them?

Be a Good Neighbor

Follow these tips so you can be a great neighbor, just like Daniel!

Tips for welcoming new neighbors

- Visit your new neighbors with a trusted adult, like a parent or caregiver, and introduce yourself. If you'd like, you can sing the welcome song at the end of this book.

- Offer to help carry or unpack the moving boxes.

- Give a small housewarming gift. You can draw a picture, pick some flowers, or bake a cake with your caregiver!

- Tell your new neighbor about your favorite places in the neighborhood, like the library or the park.

- Don't visit your new neighbors for too long. They are very busy settling into their new home. You can always visit again another time!

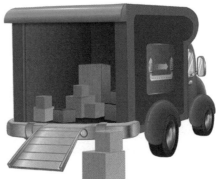

Where Would You Like to Move?

Daniel imagined that he moved to a new place. He imagined moving to a tree house, a farm, and the moon!

If you moved, where would you like to live? On a separate piece of paper, draw a picture of your new home and your new neighborhood. Here are some questions to get you started:

- Do you live in a city, in a town, or in the countryside?

- Is your neighborhood near the ocean?

- Is your neighborhood near the mountains?

- Does your neighborhood have a Main Street?

- Does it snow in your neighborhood?

- What color is your house?

- Does your house have a yard?

- How many rooms are in your house?

- Who lives with you?

- Do you have any pets?

Daniel's Welcome Song

Daniel likes to sing a song to his new neighbors to make them feel at home. You can also sing this song to a new classmate, a visitor, or anyone else you want to welcome!

We welcome you, we welcome you,
we welcome you today!
We hope you like our neighborhood.
We welcome you today!